HIDDEN RIPPLES
Life's Unspoken Language

Also by Lemuel LaRoche

Tree of Life: The Human Ascension

HIDDEN RIPPLES
Life's Unspoken Language

LEMUEL LAROCHE

Athens, Georgia

Published in United States by

LEMUEL'S INK
P.O. Box 48911
Athens, GA 30604
www.lemuellaroche.com

Copyright © 2013 by Lemuel LaRoche

All rights reserved.

Hidden Ripples: Life's Unspoken Language © Lemuel LaRoche,

No part of this book may be used, reproduced or transmitted in any form or by any means, electronic or mechanical, including photocopy, recording, or any information storage or retrieval system, without the written permission, excepting the case of brief quotation in critical article or reviews.

Author Photo: Solestential Studio, LLC
Book Editor: Michelle Castleberry, Britney LaRoche
Cover Design: HoremHeb Ankh Atum

ISBN 978-0-9884672-3-1 (paperback)

Dedication

As branches fall from the tree, new leaves blossom to celebrate life and carry on the root's wisdom. The cycle will carry on.

This book is dedicated to the memory of my grandmother, Rose Dickerson, my grandfather, Bruce L. LaRoche, and my father, William A. Taylor. The wisdom you all shared will carry on for many generations.

This book is also dedicated to all the beautiful new leaves on my family tree: Miylad & Khalida, I'mon, Akilah, Alivia, Max, Sarah, Khalid, Noah, Jasaiyah and Lemuel. May life shower you all with early wisdom. May you all find your purpose and contribute wonders into this world. May the wisdom shared in this book be carried with you along your journey.

CONTENTS

Prologue

Once in Every Life   9

The Seven Dresses   12

The Farmer's Daughter   18

A Cycle of Greed   29

Failed Mission   37

Purpose   56

Once in Every Life

By my father,
William A. Taylor

A tender, sweet, and innocent leaf was about to fall from a tree. It was not ready to go, but it was sad for lack of understanding. No one had taken the time out to explain to it what it was created to do. Seeing all other leaves about her falling gracefully, she lamented until a breeze came with comfort.

"Why are you ...crying so?" asked the breeze.

The tender sweet innocent leaf answered, "I am about to fall and I am afraid." The Breeze who was very understanding sat and comforted the leaf.

"It will not be painful for you," said the breeze. He spoke, "For if you stay the winter and survive, you will not make it through the awaiting arms of spring. You have made so many happy and so your Creator wants you to rest until it's time to bring joy again."

The leaf listened, for it had never heard its function before.

"Your mother, the tree will await your return in spring, dear leaf, and she will smile. For this is the decree of the Source of All."

A small tear fell from the eye of the leaf, for it was so happy. "Does that mean I won't be forgotten?" asked the leaf. "Yes," replied the breeze, getting ready to go.

The leaf asked of the breeze, "In what manner will I depart?"

The breeze replied, "You can leave with me." So the leaf awaited the tender breath and touch of the breeze. The leaf gracefully fell to earth's floor, but with a full overstanding, and praising the Source of All.

Hidden Ripples: Once in Every Life

The Seven Dresses

By my mother,
Pam LaRoche Proudfoot

*In this world,
materialism is the fabric of man.
This is the wisdom that was passed down to me.*

It was a bittersweet day. We'd just buried my grandmother who was ninety-six years old. Looking at her beautiful face, garbed in white, she looked at peace. No stress, no wrinkles, just peaceful; but that's the way she carried herself in life and beyond.

The tea kettle started to give a soft soothing whistle, and the rain was gently hitting the window pane. I walked around looking at her small, humble abode. No TV, just a radio, plants, sofa, table, and a small garden in the backyard. She used to say, "If anyone ever broke into my home, once they looked around, humph, they might leave me something." *Jokes, always jokes.* And we'd laugh.

Looking into her bedroom takes me back to when I was a child, spending my summers with her. One day, as I looked into her big empty closet, I said, "Grandma where are all your clothes?"

She said, "That's it. Count them for me Habibi," and I counted all the way to seven.

"Grandma, you only have seven dresses? Why? Are you poor?"

She laughed, "No baby. There are seven days in a week and I put on a clean dress every day. You may not understand now, but someday you will."

I walked into her bedroom and ran my hand across the quilt we made together. On top of the pillows, there was a letter with my name on it.

I sat down at the table with two cups of tea, and placed one in front of her chair. I could hear her voice as I read my letter:

Habibi,

By the time you read this letter, I will already be on my journey. If you look into the closet, the 8th dress on the left hand side has an envelope with $50,000 in the pocket.

Ha! Knew I couldn't fool you, bet you didn't even get up! Seven dresses, right (yes, I still have jokes)?

By now I'm laughing and crying. Yes, jokes until the end.

Habibi, let me pass you some jewels I lived by. You asked me as a child, why seven dresses. This is why....

Seven dresses kept my life simple. We waste so much time chasing after fads and wanting more and more. More of what we can't afford and don't need. Trying to keep up, and getting depressed and in debt, when we can't. It's not worth it. When you get something new, give something away. Keep it balanced.

I visit young people in the hospital with high blood presser, diabetes, and heart disease. Why? Because they eat crap. Bad diet. If you can't pronounce it or don't grow it, don't eat it.

I grow most of my food, not just because it's healthier, but when you put your hands in the earth you connect to it in more ways than one.

Folks use to call Mr. Jones's son a thug. I didn't. I saw something in his eyes. One day I asked him to move some barrels for me and we started talking and working the earth together. When he saw those seeds sprouting, you would have thought he won the lottery. He realized what his hands could be used for and he was a changed man. He'd come everyday and weed and water and just stare off into the garden, watching it grow, and I was staring at him, watching him grow. Last year was our best harvest, and we passed it out to our neighbors. Now, they look at him with respect. He even brought his wife and son around, got them digging in the dirt, too. She learned how to can and make preserves and gives it to the daycare and community center. Reach one, teach one. His family is an asset to the community. See what planting seeds will do? We were rooted together and you never know what new seeds will sprout up.

Walk, darling. It'll keep your mind clear and your body strong.

Read, read, read! Read to yourself, read to children. Teach them to love books. It can take them anywhere and they can be anything.

Give of yourself. Always be an example of grace and beauty.

Listen to nothing and you'll hear everything. You'll hear the words of the Most High in his creation. How are you going to hear Him if you're always plugged into something? Do you think He's going to send you a text? Listen to what people are saying in their eyes. Their eyes say more than words.

Get back to simplicity, get in touch with yourself.

Finally, all these jewels will give you inner joy. Even when you appear to have nothing, you'll have it all. See, I told you I wasn't poor.

Well, beloved, it's almost time for me to go. I don't want to be late for my own funeral. Tell Mr. Jones's son to start the community garden. Yes, that's a great idea. Help him out if you can and keep planting those seeds! He gets it.

Habibi, I'm leaving you my tea set and this house. I'll be in touch, just listen.

Much love,
Grandma

As the rain fell in her garden, the teardrops fell into my cup. These were not tears of sorrow. No, not sorrow. Tears of joy.

I sat thinking about the clutter and baggage that suffocated my life, and about the peace I craved. I could feel her sitting across from me smiling. She was at peace, and so was I. Just like the seeds she planted and nourished, I too felt a new growth emerging within my shell. And I just sat there and listened.

My Mom called a few hours later and asked if I was ok. "Never better," I said. "I'm going to go home and pick out my seven dresses."

Hidden Ripples: The Seven Dresses

The Farmer's Daughter

His great-grandfather was a farmer.
His grandmother was a farmer.
His father was a farmer.
He left his farm to chase the magnetic lights
shining in the cold city.
He starved to death,
but his gifts lived on!

His great-great grandfather was a farmer who possessed an extra-ordinary gift. Once a year, at the peak of summer, after the last leaf matured for the season, he would challenge himself to a thirteen-day fast. He drank only water to keep himself hydrated from the summer heat, and chewed the many herbs provided by the forest. He whispered his secret to a passing butterfly: "After the ninth day of fasting, my body gears into a numb cocoon-like state, similar to the process you encountered during your metamorphosis. When my body reaches this stage, I am no longer in control of my flesh, for I've become a passive observer."

By the thirteenth day, he could hear and feel the heartbeat of the forest roots pounding through his bare feet. He would then follow the thumping beat to the center of the forest, place his palms on the oldest tree he found and, for the next seven days, chant the names of every leaf that blossomed in the forest during that spring season.

When the fall winds arrived to carry the falling leaves along their journey, they all shared the great miracles they'd witnessed with the insects and rodents they encountered in the forest, as well as the sacred ground they landed upon. Their stories and testimonies spread quickly throughout the region and inspired the trees and the clay of the earth to agree upon a sacred vow: *As long as the trees' roots were clutched inside of Mother Earth's clay, the descendants of this man would be shielded from famine and protected from natural disaster.* The vow proved to be a sacred covenant, for in the dry seasons when insects and animal passersby raided the crops of nearby farms, his harvest was left untouched.

At dusk of each day, he powwowed with insects and animals that strolled freely onto his farm. Rumors described a council meeting held at his farm, where he chuckled with the animals and insects as they discussed the hidden comedy and dramas unfolding daily within the forest. He informed them that the human races were also filled with strange characters, and they laughed while watching the sunset. Those insects and animals that arrived from distant forests shared the stories they heard from relatives describing this man's gift and how his family name was echoed and adored throughout the region.

*

    His great-grandmother was a farmer, also endowed with an exceptional gift. Whenever the fall season visited the Earth, she devoted her time forming a personal relationship with each seed gathered from the previous harvest. She soaked every seed she intended to plant in the coming spring in the saliva beneath her tongue, allowing the intellect within the seed to fuse with her DNA. In this way, they developed a healthy connection. She became one in essence with each seed. Once this ritual was completed, she placed the seeds in a jar filled with warm water, a hint of chlorophyll and filled the atmosphere with spiritual hymns so the seeds would vibrate peacefully through the winter season. With every tone and every vibration, she thanked the seed for its purpose in life's continuous cycle.
    Some labeled her a lunatic, for rumor had it that on her farm, in the evening before the coming rain, she sung to the full crow moon while dancing with bare feet. On the day of planting, she walked the fertile field, allowing the soil to make the silent communication and connection through her. After burying the seeds deep inside of the earth, they shared the passionate message of love she encoded within them. The fertile soil received it, creating warm friction underground. During the

feast of the first spring rain, the earth exploded with the nutrients of life and sent forth from its bosom fruits, herbs, and vegetation in abundance.

*

His grandmother was a wise old farmer, blessed with unique healing powers. She developed a reputation in and around town as the bush doctor. Locals of her town would bring their dying plants to her for rejuvenation. She was employed by farmers throughout the region to help revitalize their dying trees and crops. Many in town confirmed that she had magic fingers. Some even believed that she held the hands of God. Her reputation detailed how she could bring dead vegetation back to life with a simple touch. When asked by the local farmers to share the secrets in her touch, she simply replied that humanity and the trees were one in spirit. She said, "Technology is crippling us to the ways of our roots, and will continue to deactivate our communication with our sacred Mother Earth, her leafy children, and our deepest self." She stopped, took a deep breath and continued, "The creator has ordained us into a unique marriage, but we have chosen to divorce from the source of our strength. We use not what the tree produces as meat and means of trade, but instead kill the trees to exchange her texture as a symbol of monetary wealth.

"We no longer hold sacred to the symbiotic wedding vow encoded inside of us. When did we forget that we inhale the oxygen given by the trees, as they inhale the carbon dioxide from our exhalation? I have no special gift," she would answer. "I only listen to the trees when they speak in silent tones, and wave back at the fluttering flowers during my morning walks. There is a life force that exists in the chlorophyll, as it does in the blood that flows through us. While meditating, I become one with that force, allowing me to smile the same joy of the leaves, cry the pain of broken branches, and share in the agony of the trees as they suffer from man and his unnatural ways. In return, the trees thank me with an abundance of oxygen and herbs as we continue to bond in love and admiration. I abide faithfully in the oath of our divine marriage."

*

His father was a farmer, also favored with a special gift. Like generations before him, he spoke the secret language of the plants and trees. They shared with him stories about his great-grandfather's weeklong meditation in the forest. He, too, spoke with the ants while planting seeds during the early spring season. He wrote poetry on the wings of butterflies and on the petals of the flowers they landed on. Each poem recited his appreciation to the Great Mother for beautifying earth's canvas with radiant colors. He danced in the spring rain, massaging the tense earth with his feet, as learned from his grandmother. The earth danced back, her rhythm amplified a silent song one could not hear, but surely feel.

It was reported that his farm alone fed an entire region during the locust invasion of the 1930s. Many laughed at him when he shared stories of how he was warned by the trees of the massive migration heading towards the region. He detailed how the ant colonies joined forces to create a huge shield around his farm. Rumors described how the locusts passed over his farm while decimating the crops of other farmers in the region. The farmers all expressed how lucky he was to be spared by the locusts' wrath. Little did they know about the sacred vow, and how the trees summoned every nesting bird in the region to assist the ants in guarding his farm during the invasion. He gave thanks to the Creator of All for sparing his farm from the invasion, and proceeded to feed the entire region with the harvest of his crops.

*

At the age of four, he walked with the ants in the forest and learned from them the extensive history passed down from their queen, of the great feast of 1930. At the age of eight, he began naming leaves in the forest and singing to the flowers in the field. At the age of ten, he summoned his first fall harvest and shared the yielding with his neighborhood friends and his school.

At the age of twelve, a television was placed in his home. His imagination was captured by the black and white programming tube that dominated his living room. At the age of fifteen, he sat paralyzed for the entire spring season watching the colorful programs on television. Scores of cardinals pecked at his window, calling him outside to cherish the beauty of nature, but the hypnotic spell from the tube seized his vision and filled it with mindless clutter and confusion.

At the age of seventeen, he began sneaking out of the farm at night to dance and dazzle with the luring energy of the nearby city. At the age of nineteen, he moved away from the protection of the farm to explore the magnetic ways of the urban jungle. At the age of thirty-three, he bore a beautiful daughter out of wedlock and named her after the garden of life- *Eden*. At the age of thirty-nine, he was granted custody of his daughter after the passing of her mother. In that same year, a recession visited his city and crashed through his job window, leaving him unemployed and eventually homeless on a cold concrete street. He drifted with his daughter through various homeless shelters in search of assistance, but found no fortune in Life's cruel hands. His daily routine consisted of waking up early, walking his daughter to school, and hunting for odd jobs. He often lamented of the cruelty tucked beneath the shadow of the city's skyline.

If only he would remember the natural abilities, veiled in the corner of his mind, cluttered by the television programming. If only he would remember the sacred vow that sat patiently at the farm awaiting his return. The strains of life grew tougher, causing him to give up his daughter for adoption. The Earth cried the entire week because of his decision. Meteorologists labeled it the worst storm of the decade. The rain flooded the city streets and subways, damaging many homes and leaving families stranded on rooftops. He promised his daughter that he would return for her once he found a job and got back on his feet. He promised her that they would one day occupy a nice home in the good section of the city. He promised her that everything would be back to normal. On last sighting of the man, he stood at the intersection of a busy interstate with a sign that read, *I will work for money or food. Please help me get my daughter back.*

*

    One summer weekend, the family that adopted Eden decided to have a picnic in the countryside. Their plan was to take a quiet break from the busy city and spend quality time in nature's beauty. On that day, Eden danced with new life to a silent song as she packed a small survival kit, preparing for the adventure. The bees also buzzed with new energy and the butterflies frolicked in jubilation to the flowers' joy. The grass and trees rejoiced to the message carried by the wind, as the family decided their picnic location for that special day.

    While the family's SUV raced from the city towards the countryside, no one in the vehicle noticed Eden's eyes: fully captured and mesmerized by the sun's glare. The adopted father activated the child lock on his vehicle to stop Eden from pulling the window down, even after commanding her not to touch the window. "What's gotten into you today", he repeated throughout the ride. Finally, the family reached their destination safely.

When Eden stepped out of the vehicle to lay her little feet on the ground, it all happened in a sudden, swift movement.

The energy of the ground called her through the rubber soles of her sneakers. She stood still with her eyes closed, downloading a language she has never heard, yet understood clearly. For she, too, possessed the hidden gift that rippled through her generations. Her spirit was captivated by nature's welcoming choir song. She heard the ants marching in a soulful unison to the forest's heartbeat, which sounded like soft drums welcoming her back to her ancestral habitat. The birds sang her name through many songs, while the trees collectively chanted and swayed in euphoria at her presence.

It was as if an invisible force controlled Eden as she began walking to the forest of her ancestors.

The family was too busy unloading the SUV of food and camping supplies to notice Eden heading towards the woods. She was only seven years old, and heard the forest's choir as clearly as her great-great-great grandfather. She felt her great-great grandmother's footprints as she unknowingly traced each step. She took her shoes off and continued walking into her trance. The beauty of the butterflies dazzled her eyes as they assisted her deeper into the forest. She followed without a care, for she felt safe, secure, at peace and at home. She talked with the ants as they chaperoned her through secret pathways deeper into the forest. The trees provided her with herbs, fruits, shelter and love as she roamed into the darkness.

Today, her picture still sits on the bulletin board in the nearest grocery store with *Missing* in bold print above her smiling face. After seven years, no one has seen the face nor heard the voice of the little girl who vanished in the forest on that bright and sunny, summer day. But the trees, the ants, and the bees of the forest shared with me a different story.

Hidden Ripples: The Farmer's Daughter

A Cycle of Greed

It is the vulture's greed, which will eventually take his life.
It is the vulture's gluttony, which will shorten his breath.
Until he learns that sharing is a sacrifice of love,
he will forever wallow in the cycle of death.

It was a scorching hot and dry August day. A lonesome black vulture soared the dehydrated sky of the Arizona desert in search of a meal. His belly ached with hunger pains as his eyes desperately combed all corners of the desert for food. It was his third day without a meal and weakness now consumed the little strength he once possessed. The hidden hand of hunger caused desperation to ripple through his thoughts, but the heavens now favored him. He watched a wounded adult male Peccary slowly limping and holding desperately to life after being struck by a speeding jeep.

The impact from the collision sent excruciating pain up the spine of the Peccary and eventually locked still his legs as he collapsed on the highway, shaking and gasping for his final breath.

The vulture witnessed the entire dramatization from the distance and quickly headed to the location of impact to investigate the scene. He soared patiently above, waiting for the reaper to shepherd away the Peccary's spirit, while observing the sky to assure that no one else was a witness to the event. He analyzed the corpse from afar. After concluding that no traps were being set by the land dwelling creatures, he zoomed down with full speed to partake of the deceased Peccary now lying in the middle of the road.

He was thankful, especially to be the only vulture on the deserted highway to gorge in this elaborate meal. He ripped into the flesh of the carcass with his beak, guzzling his tongue with the blood of the road kill. He paused for a brief second, looked around to see if there were any cars, coyotes or other vultures in sight. When realizing that he was alone on this desolate highway, he continued in devouring the carcass as fast as he could.

Sharing was not on his agenda today. The very thought of being spotted by other vultures clouded his judgment as he continued to chow, barely giving himself time for small breaths and the enjoyment of his meal. From a distance, he heard the rumbling sound of a car's engine approaching. He stopped eating, and lifted his head to inspect the sound. He fixed his vision to examine the noise and the direction it came from. He locked his eyes on the moving object he saw in the distance of the blazing summer heat.

A vehicle was heading towards him at full speed, but his mind was attentive to his meal. Using his eyes and his keen accuracy in math, he calculated his distance from the speeding car to be exactly two miles. *Two miles is a century away to the crawling ants. I could finish this road kill before the car arrives*, he thought, and proceeded in his selfish feast. He continued to eat as if it was his last supper. The roaring engine sound grew louder and closer. Again, he lifted his head to recalculate his distance to the car.

He stared at the coming vehicle for a brief second more and fell into a deep thought: *Should I fly away to safety, or continue ingesting this carcass?* He understood clearly the danger of flirting with death after watching the reaper carry away the spirit of his current meal.

He recalled countless examples and casualties of those rodents who chanced with death on the highway of life. They, too, had provided him with many meals. He reflected on all the stories he had heard of close family members that lost their lives on the same highway. He knew that his first thought of flying away to safety was the most reasonable, but the second thought was more satisfying for his gluttonous nature.

He entertained his second thought vigorously and continued to gorge at the road kill. He felt the ground vibrating for his attention. He could feel the car speeding closer to him, but he ignored the warning. His mind was set on satisfying the tapeworms in his stomach, and so he ate faster as if no meals were promised tomorrow. He wanted desperately to finish this road kill before any other vulture would locate him and join in the feast. He did not wish to share this meal with anyone today.

As the ground trembled harder, the vulture ate faster. He could see from the corner of his eyes the car approaching with raging speed. He looked up for a quick second to measure his distance from the vehicle. He calculated twelve seconds before the car was to reach his exact location. Only twelve seconds to avoid impact. He timed it perfectly in his head: *I'll eat for eight more seconds and then fly away.*

He proceeded with his plan, looking up and down in between every bite to avoid a collision. The car raced closer and closer to him, as he continued to eat faster. Finally, he flew away, timing it just right. The car missed him by a half second as he escaped death's silent touch. *That was close,* he thought to himself. He felt the sun's heat blazing off the car, only inches from his wings.

He was caught in the speeding drag of the car and slowly regained his momentum. It took a few minutes for him to fully recover his balance. He then proceeded back to the spot of the dead carcass and continued where he left off. He ate alone and undisturbed for several minutes until his belly was full. He stopped eating, took a deep breath and glanced at his surroundings to assure that he wasn't being watched. From the far distance, he could see another vulture heading towards him in full speed. He calculated his distance from the approaching vulture to be exactly four miles. Although his belly was full of food, and there was enough left over to feed two more vultures, gluttony dominated his thoughts. He focused his attention back to the dead carcass, and continued to overindulge in his meal. He ate with excruciating speed, refusing to share this road kill with anyone.

His legs began to shake from the trembling ground. He quickly glanced up and spotted a bigger vehicle heading his way. He then gazed in the opposite direction to locate the distance of the approaching vulture. He calculated both the distance of the vehicle and the vulture to be two miles away. *Only a few more bites and I'll be done with this carcass*, he thought.

He continued eating the road kill as fast as he could, looking up every few seconds to time his distance from the vehicle. He felt the vibration on the ground growing stronger, but continued eating. He could also now hear in the wind the flapping wings of the arriving vulture. He ate faster and faster as the vehicle proceeded closer and closer. Finally, he stuffed his mouth with the last piece of dead flesh scraped from the road while locking his eyes on the vehicle only twenty inches from his bloody beak.

He tried flying away as quickly as he could, only to find that his body had become too heavy of a burden on his wings. An extra sixty pounds was not so easy to haul. If only he was molded like an ant to carry ten times his body weight, or fashioned like a camel to store six hundred pounds on his back, but he was a vulture that thought with his stomach and not his mind. His plumped belly instantly affected his speed. He mustered all the strength he could command, but overeating had put an uneasy amount of pressure on him, making it difficult to lift his wings and carry his heavy body.

The wind shared a silent eulogy, as the head of the vulture collided with the bumper of the pick up truck, sending his body into a three hundred sixty degree spinning motion. Small increments of his life flashed in his mind before it faded into black. The impact from the collision claimed the vulture's final breath. He became the road kill he once devoured, and now lay lifeless in the middle of the highway as a testament of greed.

When the other vulture arrived to the scene, he maintained his distance to allow the reaper his moment of passage. He then walked near the dead carcass. He stood still in the middle of the empty highway to catch his breath from the flight. He glanced around in all directions of the sky to see if any other vultures were in sight. He studied his surroundings to assure that no land creatures were preparing a trap. After noticing that he was alone on this highway, he quickly began devouring the road kill. He ate with speed hoping to finish his meal before being spotted by any other vultures.

He was halfway through his meal, when he felt the ground vibrating. He looked up and saw at the distance, an eighteen-wheeler truck heading his way. He calculated his distance to the truck at five miles. "I can finish this meal before the vehicle reaches me", he mumbled quietly. He was almost done with his meal, so he put his head back down and continued gorging the flesh of the dead carcass left in the middle of the road.

Hidden Ripples: A Cycle of Greed

Failed Mission

*The power of words and thoughts
can inspire great wonders,
as well as great destruction.
One can never hide from his true self.*

It was a humid day in July and the playground of Spring Grove Apartments was filled with laughter, the sound of crickets singing summer lullabies, and children enjoying their summer break from school. The foul smell sailing from the open kitchen window of Apartment 23 attracted hundreds of flies to feast on the bags of garbage left there that hadn't been emptied in weeks. While the flies were filling their hairy bellies with the leftover trash, the entire Roach clan was journeying from all corners of a kitchen cabinet. They were in route to their sacred meeting place in the center of the cabinet, which sat directly above the stove.

The clan's chief, Elda, was pacing back and forth on the rooftop of a salt container with one hand on his back and the other hand slowly stroking his long gray beard. He was preparing to give an elaborate speech. As he downloaded the details of his speech through his antenna, the various clans were making their way towards their selected seats.

Chief Elda's antenna rose to a unique position, signaling that the entire clan was seated and prepared for the meeting. He stopped, stood still from his pacing, and gazed into the audience. He raised both arms and the clan immediately replied with a dead silence.

He spoke with his usual wise words and calm demeanor. Chief Elda said, "It has been many moons since we met and feasted together as a clan. I send forward my warmest greeting to the Nor-Roach clan of the Northern walls, my love to the So-Roach clan of the Southern walls, my admiration to the Ea-Roach clan of the Eastern walls, and my best regards to the We-Roach clan of the Western walls." The entire clan responded in a collective rhythm to greet their great chief. All roaches were present with their antennae standing at attention, preparing to download the urgent message their chief was to deliver.

Chief Elda spoke again: "I called this meeting to address two dire concerns which are related in nature. The elders of each clan have shared with me their unsettled anxiety, and we have telepathically communicated about their daunting concerns in great length.

"Take a look around you my children. Our population has grown by sixty-seven percent since our last meeting. We are afraid that if we continue at this rapid rate of growth, we will outgrow our sacred village within seven months' time." A wave of noise erupted within the audience. The clan of roaches began holding smaller group conversations amongst each other, discussing and translating the news they had just received. Chief Elda raised his arms for silence and it was granted instantly.

He continued in a softer tone: "I've been having strange dreams lately about a famine, an extermination of some sort that is to visit our clan. In these dreams, many have perished from chemical warfare. I tried ignoring and downplaying these dreams as senseless nightmares, but they have continued to haunt me in my realm of sleep and my waking state. When I informed the wise council of these dreams, I became more alarmed when I learned that similar dreams had visited and haunted other elders in the village."

The quiet room became active with small chatter about the chief's dream and concerns of the elders. Chief Elda glanced at his wise council, lifted his arms and the room fell quiet once again.

He proceeded, "I, along with selected elders and the wise council, have been meeting over the last few weeks to discuss these dreams in full length, and to design a plan forward for the entire clan. As a result of these meetings, we have agreed that if we wish to escape this famine or extermination soon to visit our clan, we must explore and migrate beyond our sacred grounds." The room roared with discussion of the latest news. The chief continued to speak above the chatter.

"In the past, we have secretly sent a few of our greatest warriors, scientists, and trackers to explore the outer boundaries out these walls, but none have returned. The mystery of the other side still haunts us today, but the time has come to face our deepest fears. There may be a great utopia that awaits us outside of these great walls, or there may be a trap set by the big foots to exterminate us." He elevated his voice louder, "But unless we dig deep within ourselves, and summon that collective courage to take that great journey and carve our footprints into the walls of history, we will never know, and we, too, will fade away in the ashes of time."

A hidden force rippled through the meeting hall, and the room fell silent with every roach's eyes and antennae locked keenly onto the great Chief.

He continued with sadness in his voice, "My children, there are those amongst us who are old enough to remember, those that survived the great famines and extermination of the past. There are those who can vividly recall when the cruel left hand of time abandoned us with no food in sight for months. Where we survived only by eating the layer of white coat that covers these walls. There is a sweet chemical in the paint that is plastered on these walls, and it has claimed the life of so many loved ones, but still, we have survived."

Shaking his balled fist, and elevating the sorrow in his voice, the chief continued with tears running down his cheek: "Our brave ancestors did what they had to do to survive, to clutch near and dear to life, so they could breathe new breath into our colony. We must never forget the devastating effects it had on our village. It shrunk our population by eighty-two percent. Each of us lost eight close relatives and a first born to that awful famine. Now we must learn from the cruel patterns of history. We must prepare ourselves to avoid the next great famine and extermination. We will survive, we will carry on!"

Those words sent a shock of optimism through the crowd as they stood to cheer the chief's strength. Chief Elda looked around the room and with his right antenna, he signaled for specific elders and the council members to stand up. He raised his arms for silence and it was received.

Pointing at the council of old and feeble roaches, he spoke with a serious tone, "Take a good look at the elders standing before you. They are your heroes. We must never forget their sacrifices. If they could withstand the torture of hunger, and survive the grave grip of death for the sake of this colony, then surely we can do the same."

The room exploded with thunderous cheers. Chief Elda continued shouting above the loud applause: "Surely, the DNA strand of resilience lives within each of us. Every roach in here was designed for greatness." He raised his arm and said with a heartfelt air, "The time has come to test that resilient strength within us once more." The room fell to complete silence.

Chief Elda continued calmly: "We need from every clan the sacrifice of one brave roach to journey outside of these walls to help set a trail of hope for our migration. The four brave roaches selected will spend two weeks in robust training in preparation of this mission. They will master their inner strength and peel away the curse of individualism to become a collective one. They will learn to lean on each others' strength, for all will complement their brothers' weakness. It will be like putting a broken puzzle together. As a unit, they will move as a solid force.

"The experts gathered from our village will skill them in the art of survival. They will acquire knowledge on the science of tracking and absorb diligently the art of camouflaging in the shadows of cracks to avoid the danger presented by the big foots. They will learn to suppress their desire when it arises. They will learn to conqueror their willpower, so that they can be prepared to overcome when they are faced with hunger and starvation. They will become brown belts in the art of hand to shell combat so they may, upon sensing trouble, disengage any insect they cross paths with.

"We have gathered a list of thousands of species, including the giants of our own species and furry creatures they may encounter outside of these walls. They will be trained on ways to avoid the army of ants, and the hungry spiders hiding in the corner of walls waiting to dispose and suck them dry. Finally, they will master the art of stillness, in case they need to stand motionless for hours, days, even weeks at a time if needed to avoid death." The Chief paused for a few seconds, stared in the crowd and continued: "The growth, the survival of our great and mighty colony will rest on the shells of these four brave roaches."

When the last words sailed from the Chief's mouth, dozens of courageous young roaches from each clan pushed and shoved each other as they ran to the forefront of the podium hoping to be selected for the mission. The crowd burst into cheers to applaud the bravery of these young roaches.

For the next few hours, the volunteers were assessed and evaluated diligently to determine their patience level, strategic insight, critical thinking exercises, and mental fitness for this somber mission of hope and survival. Out of the forty-eight brave roaches that volunteered, four roaches were selected as the best fit for the mission. The clan elders formed a small circle around the four and showered them with their earnest blessings before bringing them to center stage to stand with Chief Elda in front of the entire village.

Chief Elda spoke with pride: "O mighty clan, these four roaches were selected as most fit from the abundance of strong and brave roaches that volunteered. We owe all that volunteered our greatest blessing and gratitude. It is because of your courage that our clan will survive the toughest of times."

Chief paused for a moment, stared at the four roaches, then continued: "Standing before you at this critical moment are the warriors that will explore and penetrate the depth of the abyss. They will determine the longevity of our survival. One was selected as a sacrifice from each clan to blaze the trail for the journey to the new world." The entire village stood on their young and old feet to cheer on their new heroes. The standing ovation sent chills down the spine of each roach selected for the mission. The chief lifted his hands for silence and then continued: "The entire village, every clan will participate in a collective meditation to build a force of protection for our brave sons to carry on their expedition. When their training is complete, we will engage in a ceremonial celebration by feasting and dancing until that great door opens." He pointed at the kitchen cabinet door. "This will be the sign and mark for the beginning of the journey."

The clan spent the next two weeks (two human days) in collective meditation and fully engaged in clan rituals. Each of the four selected roaches' bags were filled with good luck ornaments from members of their particular clan, along with a heap of helpful items to carry on the mission. The chief walked into the crowded cabinet and commanded the attention of the entire clan. He smiled as a proud father would after watching his child complete a tough task.

The audience watched with delighted eyes as the chief prepared to speak. "O mighty clan, the training is complete." The crowd burst into cheers, tears, and began hollering the names of the roach representing their particular clan. The chief brought the roaches out and they were all given a special ornament for protection from the village elders. The Chief raised his arms and the room fell to silence. "O mighty roaches let us celebrate our new beginning. Sound the alarms, let the festivities begin." Drums and various unique instruments were brought out and the dancing, singing and partying geared into full motion. They drank and danced in soulful unison, showing and giving thanks to and for the brave roaches.

The party proceeded for several nights. They feasted in high spirit, drank and laughed in blissful energy for weeks on out.

Everything came to a crucial halt in a swift instant. Silence partook the clan, as they stood frozen watching the giant door as it opened slowly. It was as if the entire scene happened in slow motion. The roaches quickly took cover as a giant hand came crashing through the party. But this was not a time for fear. This was the sign they had all waited for. This was the moment that determined the lifeline of generations to come. This was the great genesis of their ultimate exploration for survival. The entire village cheered with great joy, while hiding to avoid being detected by the giant hand.

The four roaches gathered their bags in a swift motion and ran carefully on the sidewall towards the main entrance of the great giant door. They hid in the corner to calculate the swinging door's motion with skillful precision and decided it was best to leap out just before the door came to a full close. Their timing was impeccable and precise. As the door came to a speeding shut, they prayed in silence and leaped out as a collective one, only for three of the four to land in a pot of boiling soup. *Failed mission...*

*

Eight hours earlier, the ringing of his cell phone awakened Alex Rudolph from his state of deep slumber. On the opposite end of the phone was a jittery voice he knew all too well. "Rise and shine my precious son. This is the world's greatest mother calling for her young scholar."

Alex sighed as if regretting picking up the phone. "Hey mom," he replied.

His mother continued, "We haven't seen you in months. How is the semester coming along?"

Alex sighed heavier, as if not wanting to carry on the conversation. "It's coming along," he replied. "So far, I'm passing all my classes with exception of biology." Alex paused for a minute while releasing a yawn into the telephone. He continued, "I'll pick it up."

"I know you will," replied his mother, "but I'm calling you with a surprise. You will never guess it."

Alex rubbed his palm across his forehead and shook his head in frustration, now realizing he shouldn't have picked up the phone. "Mom, it's too early. I promise I'll call you when I wake up."

"Did you work late last night?" continued his mother.

"Yes, and I just need a few more hours," replied Alex sarcastically.

"Ok, ok," replied his mother, knowing that he was rushing her off the phone. "I'll let you go in a second. I just want you to know that your brother is out of school until Wednesday and I've requested time off this week. With the time off, I figured it's important for him to spend some time down there and see what college life is like. As I'm speaking, we are loading the car and we'll be pulling out in an hour. We wanted to surprise you, but I wasn't sure if you'd be working today."

"Ok mom. I'll see you soon." Alex rushed to hang up the phone as if he did not hear a word that was shared by his mother. He dozed off again for about thirty seconds. His body began twitching as if haunted by a nightmare, and a burst of energy forced his once sleepy eyes open. He quickly pulled the blanket from his head and jerked his back to upright position. Everything that was said finally came crashing into his mind. *My mother is coming!* He jumped out of bed and stared at his filthy room in panic. He immediately called his mother back to assure that he heard her correctly. "Mom, did you say you and Moses were coming to visit today?"

"Yes," replied his mother in her usual jittery voice. "We hope to be there before sunset. Be sure to..." Alex moved the phone from his ears to take a quick peek at the clock on his phone, and cringed at the time. He brought the phone back to his ears to catch his mother finishing off her statement. "...and teach your brother about appropriate hygiene. His room is a mess. He wears the same pants for days at a time. I need you to talk to him."

Rushing to get her off the phone once again, Alex replied, "Ok mom, I'll talk to him when you all get here. Let me get up, brush my teeth, and get my day started. Call me when you get close so I can guide you in."

"No need for that," replied his mother. "This GPS is really good. I borrowed it from your aunt Helen. She said..."

Alex interrupted her, "Mom, I'll see you soon. You can tell me all about it later."

"Ok," replied his mother. "I'll see you in a few hours. I'll call you when I'm close." She hung up the phone.

Alex looked around his filthy room once more and shook his head in disappointment. He took a few deep breaths, threw on the first piece of clothes he laid his eyes on and ran into the kitchen towards the trash bags. He picked up the loads of full garbage bags piled against the kitchen wall, which released dozens of flies. Alex swung at the flies to guide them out of the window, shutting it before running down the stairs to place the garbage bags in the trunk of his car. He hurtled up and down the steps until all the garbage bags were out of his apartment. He ran up the stairs one last time to grab his wallet and headed out of the door. He sped with slight caution to the entrance of the apartment to dump the garbage bags in the dumpster, and raced down to the nearest supermarket.

He parked his vehicle, grabbed a shopping cart and sprinted inside of the store to begin shopping. He loaded his shopping cart with cleaning supplies, clothes detergent, breakfast items, and dinner he planned to cook that evening for his mother and brother. After paying for all of his items, he bolted as fast as he could out of the store to load the groceries into his car.

He raced back to his apartment, unloaded the groceries, and began cleaning. Assessing the filth of his apartment, he knew it would take hours to clean, wash his loads of dirty clothes, and cook dinner.

He began to verbally chastise himself, regretting how he'd allowed the junk to build up to this point. "I have to do better than this," he said to himself. "I have to set a better example for my brother." His mind flashed with images of his mother's disappointed face. His ears rang with her nagging voice fussing about how filthy he had become, how she had taught him better than that, and what a bad example he was for his brother.

Alex quickly snapped out of his daydream and began hap hazardously cleaning the kitchen. He placed all of his stained pots, cups, and dishes that had been left untouched in the sink for weeks into the dishwasher. He wiped clean all the filth piled up on the stove and counter onto the floor. He cleaned the oven and removed all of the old breadcrumbs that fell to the bottom from long ago pizza-warming nights. He swept and mopped the kitchen floor, opened the windows to release more flies, and then proceeded to his bedroom.

For the next few hours, he cleaned his room thoroughly. He loaded and unloaded the washer and dryer so that his family would have clean sheets, blankets and towels to use. Fully aware that he was racing against time, Alex began to pick up his pace. His mind was haunted by the reputation he knew he had to uphold with his mother and the example she believed he must set for his younger brother. As Alex began vacuuming his living room, his cell phone rang, stopping him in his tracks.

The warm, but jittery voice of his mother on the other line said, "We are less than two hours away and traffic seems a bit heavy. Your brother and I are getting hungry, but I refuse to stop because I would prefer not to drive in the dark. You know I have difficulty seeing at night. You know how bad my eyes are…"

Alex removed the phone from his ears and took a few deep breaths. He tried remaining calm and patient with his mother. He knew that if he did not interject, his mother would hold his ear hostage with the phone until she arrived. He made several attempts of interjecting and taking back control of the conversation, but it was too late. His mother was in full speed, going from one topic to another.

He placed his phone on mute so that his mother could not hear him vacuuming. Every time he stopped to vacuum another part of the living room, he unmuted the phone and responded with his usual *uh huh, mmmm,* and fake chuckle to give the impression that he was listening. He decided to boldly interrupt his mother. "Mom, my battery is about to die. I have to put it on the charger so it can be fully charged to buzz you into the complex."

His mother continued, "Before you hang up, I hope you still remember those cooking lessons I taught you. Now is the time to show your Momma those skills. I want you to fix us some dinner. I wanted to take you out to eat, but you know I don't like driving at night. You know how bad my eyes get at night. I don't..."

"Mom," Alex interrupted with a stern voice to stop her before she got started again. "I have to charge my phone."

"Ok sweetie. I'll see you soon." Alex hung up his phone and finished vacuuming the living room. He proceeded to the bathroom, scrubbing it thoroughly to remove the rings around the tub and toilet.

Alex headed to the kitchen to begin cooking dinner. He washed his hands, pulled out a big pot from the dishwasher, and filled it with chicken and vegetable broth. He pulled out some vegetables from the refrigerator and rinsed them thoroughly in a bowl, placing them on the side near the pot. He removed the cutting board and knives from the drawer near the sink and began cutting up some onions, potatoes, garlic, carrots and other vegetables for the soup.

While cutting the vegetables, he checked off the long to-do list in his mind. "I know I'm forgetting something," he repeated to himself. "What am I forgetting?" He placed a lid on the broth and allowed it to cook. He pulled out the garlic bread roll from the refrigerator, put extra butter on it, and wrapped it with aluminum foil before placing it in the oven. He was sure not to put the oven on. He didn't want the bread to burn before his family arrived.

He sent a text to his younger brother to calculate their distance from the house. After about five minutes, his brother replied that they were less than an hour away. Alex put the stove on low to allow the broth to simmer, and proceeded to take a quick shower to freshen up.

Before ironing his clothes, he closed all the windows in the house and put the oven on low to allow the aroma of the garlic bread to fill the house. He ironed his clothes and began getting dressed, knowing that at any moment his doorbell would ring. He walked from room to room with a thought plaguing his mind. "I'm forgetting something. What is it?"

Ding dong, the doorbell rang. He inhaled deeply, and released to prepare his mind for the experience. He breathed one last sigh of relief before opening the door to meet his mother and younger brother. They locked into each other's arms to exchange hugs. He kissed his mother on her cheeks, and punched his brother's arms before drawing him closer for another hug. He helped his mother unload her car with bags of little trinkets she brought from home.

"That garlic bread sure smells good," his mother complimented in a friendly voice. She continued, "As hungry as I am, I think I can eat an entire roll by myself." He forced a fake laugh out while watching his younger brother roll his eyes to the ceiling and shake his head as he stood behind his mother. Alex gave his little brother a quick tour around the house and ran to the kitchen to turn off the oven and remove the garlic bread roll. He prepared the dining room table and sat his family around it. He proceeded to the kitchen to prepare the meal. He cut the garlic bread into three huge slices and placed them on a plate. Next, he took the lid off the pot of broth and tasted it before serving it. The soup was bland. He thought to himself, *All that running around I was doing caused me to forget the most important ingredients. I forgot to season the soup.* He opened the kitchen cabinet door to get the salt, pepper, and seasoning salt.

He saw a few roaches running through the cabinet. He quickly looked back to assure that his mother wasn't watching. It was as if the world moved in slow motion. Just as he was closing the cabinet door, he helplessly watched four defiant and brave roaches diving head first into his pot of soup. Three landed in the soup, while one gripped himself to the pot, ran to the outside, and jumped off to hide in the crack of the oven. Alex swung wildly to kill the roach. He grew heated with frustration. Now he could not serve his family the soup. *Another failed mission...*

*

The following Tuesday after his family headed back home, Alex purchased three cans of Raid and thoroughly sprayed the entire kitchen cabinet, killing all roaches in sight and bringing the chief's dream into fruition. Despite the massive extermination of the roaches, the clan lives on.

Hidden Ripples: Failed Mission

Purpose

Never doubt or surrender the power within you.
For as the sun shines with luminous purpose;
The blue ocean waves with calm purpose;
The trees stand in purpose;
Also, the mosquito has a purpose.

The Queen saw the article while looking through her crystal ball. The title read: *Top Scientists Will Test Water Supply in Zimbabwe.* The article covered less than a quarter portion of the page and sat lonely in the bottom right corner of page 8b of the World in Scope newspaper. Only those readers whose hobbies were reading the entire newspaper saw the tiny article and like many other stories before this one, they shoved it in the back of their minds where they buried the rest of the worthless news fed to them daily.

"Funny how things can be hidden in plain sight," murmured the Queen. She was an old and wise bee, only one of three remaining unique Queen Bees in the entire southern region of Africa. She stared into her crystal and watched the entire episode unfold before her. She smiled as she placed her small crystal in the petal of a Ghaap and said in a soft whisper, "Humans, when will they ever learn?"

Approximately one hundred and sixty miles southeast of the Queen, a young and inquisitive mosquito named Farai was flying through the bushes of Mutare in Zimbabwe with her head low and her eyes staring at the pond.

From the perception of the insects flying adjacent to her, she appeared to be very low in spirit, and high in sadness. Farai landed on a leaf in a pond and stared into the water. She stared at her reflection, hoping it would relieve the gloom that coated the cloud hovering above her. In her eyes were tears of despair and her spirit was cloaked in the cocoon of sorrow. Her mind was filled with many questions about the missing pieces to life's puzzle. All that flew above her knew the state of sadness she dwelled in, and chose not to dampen their day with her clouds.

A passing wise elder mosquito named Mukai spotted the dispirited young mosquito sitting on the pond, drowning in her mind. She joined her for conversation and hoped that her wisdom would rejuvenate life back into the eyes of the young mosquito. "Why do you choose to sit on this pond of joy with so much sadness," asked the elder Mukai.

Farai shook her head from left to right and shrugged her shoulder acknowledging Mukai's words, but choosing not to engage in the conversation.

"What's your name?" asked Mukai.

"My name is Farai, I am the daughter of Farirai and Scova," answered Farai in a low tone.

"Farai!" repeated Mukai, "Well, you sure are not living up to glory of your name. My mother was named Farai because of the many smiles she shared with the world as a larva. Your name carries meaning," she continued. "And with a name like Scova, I know your proud and wise father taught you to always make eye contact with your elders and flap your little wings with pride."

Farai lifted her head to make eye contact and replied, "My father with all of his pride and wisdom flew away to meet the city lights, never to return. My mother met her destiny on the arm of a two-legger leaving me all alone to solve the hidden puzzles of life. How proud must I be by their examples and fate?" She placed her head low again to face the water.

Mukai pondered in silence for a few seconds and then shared, "Farai, we are mirrors, reflections of our loved ones in present and pass. We are also a likeness of each other. When other insects in the bush see a mosquito sitting alone in the pond with her head facing the water, that mosquito becomes a reflection of our entire species."

Farai lifted her head to make eye contact with elder Mukai again. Mukai continued to speak in her wisdom. "When I was a larva coming into age, my elders shared how important it was to walk and fly with my head and spirit high, so that I would be able to see all the beautiful colors the world wanted to show me, and experience everything the world wanted to share. It is a hidden code ingrained on the shores of every mosquito's heart that we must fly with pride, fill the sky with our sweet buzzing melody and show the other insects in the bush that we were fashioned a proud species."

Farai replied in an unhappy tone, "I cannot pretend to feel something that I do not. Besides, who cares what the other insects think about us? Who cares about the many colors the world wants to share? Surely, when fall visits with cold hands upon the earth, all the colors will fall and fade away like my mothers and fathers before me."

Mukai stared at Farai with puzzling eyes, trying to read her energy and understand the root to her thoughts. The elder was also shocked to hear a younger mosquito speak with old wisdom and rejecting the wisdom she was offering. "Share with me, and this ancient pond the thoughts that grapple with your young spirit," demanded Mukai.

Farai replied, "I feel empty and alone inside, like a vase that sits in the home of the two-leggers. I question the patterns of life, and I'm curious to know its hidden hands that simultaneously affect us all. What is it that life has in store for me? What is it that she has to offer? What must I strive to attain and live for, while amongst the leaves, bees and ants? I sit everyday staring in the pond hoping that one day this pond will show me my true purpose for being. Show me my destiny so that I may fly and sing to life with dignity and honor. But instead, my curiosity goes unfilled, and life's mystery becomes a cavernous sensation with every minute I sit near this pond. What purpose is our species on this planet? These are the daunting questions haunting my ideas, and with every ripple fading in this pond, I grow more inquisitive of my purpose here."

Mukai stroked the tip of her proboscis with one hand, while twirling her left antenna with the other. She stared to the sky as if searching for signs and an answer from a passing cloud.

Farai continued, "Why would the Great and Divine Molder form our species? What purpose do we have in a whirlpool of bugs? Are we fashioned only to fly around and sup the blood off the two and four-leggers in our midst? To eat has even become a mission of life and death for our species.

"Who would orchestrate such a tragedy for which we must act out? I barely escaped with my life from the swinging tail of a wildebeest in the morning. To eat is to dance with death during every meal. Is this divine comedy for all to laugh upon? For I stopped laughing in the passing of mother Farirai, and I've tried exploring the inner layers of my thoughts while staring into yesterday's moon. What is there to be proud of?" she repeated in a low tone.

The elder Mukai leveled her eyes to meet with Farai's. In her eyes was the answer she searched for. It sprang up in her mental reservoir, and she was ready to share. She answered, "Is not the wildebeest a prey of the lion while grazing the field? They too must eat with life's cautious touch. Are the lions not prey of the two-leggers that hold the loud instruments of power? And are the two-leggers not prey of lions and every other bloodthirsty predator in the Serengeti? Every breathing creature must walk the earth with vigilance, for death follows behind with two steps. More importantly, I understand clearly the matter that holds your young spirit. I know exactly what troubles you in this moment of your development. May I guess your age, are you sixteen or seventeen weeks young?"

Mukai's guess captured Farai's attention. Farai replied, "I'm seventeen weeks young, how do you know this?"
"Ahhh," Mukai whispered while shaking her head, "I wish your father Scova had warned you of the pupa stage before exploring into the city. This inquiring moment of your youth will pass you soon. You are experiencing what our wise elders call the Age of Wings. The Age of Wings peaks at nineteen weeks young for most mosquitoes, but some discover it earlier. You are near the

age where we lose the majority of our young mosquitos from the bush to the luminous chaos of the metropolis; for much of the same queries that you are currently describing."

She continued to share the disheartening statistic, "Some estimate that we lose over a hundred thousand mosquitoes an hour in the metropolis jungle. Our youth explore our mighty continent and some return with ancient and sacred wisdom from afar, while others never make it back home to warn the young of their ominous plight. Very little return as noble, proud and dignified mosquitoes. Many become slaves to the shimmering city, never to be seen again."

The elder saw a glimpse of light in Farai's eyes. She feared that she'd just sparked her adventurous spirit, but understood that her odyssey was inevitable. Mukai was thankful that she was at least able to guide Farai along her journey with a particular path and purpose. "I will give you an address to the Great Queen Bee of Harare. I want you to seek her and share with her your dire questions and thoughts. She is indeed a great oracle of wisdom. It was she that guided me to clarity when I struggled during my Age of Wings. I must warn you that it is a three to four day journey depending on your strength and speed. There will be many diversions along the way, and I pray that you remain focused on your task without becoming distracted by the clutter and disarray you will surely encounter."

The elder scribbled the address to the Queen's hive on a small piece of leaf and gave it to Farai. Farai tucked it in her left wing pocket and stood to stare at the elder Mukai with a new sense of purpose burning through her pupils. She thanked the elder Mukai for being patient and sharing her abundance of wisdom. The two mosquitoes embraced one another with goodbye hugs and a hand gesture common to mosquitoes, and flew away in separate directions.

Farai departed from Mukai, her mind was now filled with a new adventure. Finally, a mission was carved before her that she believed would open the many doorways inside of her. She was determined to meet the Queen Bee of Harare. But before heading away on her journey, she wanted to stop by her resting place to retrieve a few items, and fare one last goodbye to her sanctuary in the bush.

While flying back home, she replayed the words of the wise elder Mukai as they sprang new excitement in her mind and spirit. Farai reached her place of peace and stared at all the clipped baby wings of her great ancestors that flew before her. Life was now an adventure and she glared at it through a new set of compound eyes. She no longer dreaded her once lonely imagination, but now sought to find answers to the many questions burning inside of her.

Farai was determined to decode and unravel the missing keys and warnings left by her father. She began recalling some of his many sayings that puzzled her: *Every young mosquito will one day touch the sunset with their minds.* Those words from her father still resonated within her, but only now could she understand them. Her life was beginning to make a little more sense. It was now sprinkled with a greater meaning, and the curiosity that once burned in her mind was finally shown a path to embark. She now understood why many members of her family voyaged away in search of the higher meaning to life's riddled questions. She confirmed in her realization that she too must journey away from the bush of Mutare, but made an oath that she would return to inspire and warn the pupas of the lessons gained from her experience. She glanced at the baby wings of her favorite uncle Tawana. She could still recall his deep baritone buzzing as he expressed how he must take a journey to the Harare, but promised to return in one flesh, as he flew away into the sunset. That was the last day she saw her uncle. She remembered stories shared by her mother, as passed down by her Great-grandmother Tadisa, and many generations prior. They told of the many journeys traveled by her ancestors to the nest of the city before the strange two-leggers arrived by sea with the luminous lights.

As she stared at the wings of her favorite cousin Tapiwai, she envisioned his round face. He was only a few weeks older than her, and had the wisdom and philosophical perspective of his father Tawana. She reminisced on his smooth buzz, boasting of how he was too strong for the city light. "The light only traps those mosquitoes without imaginations", he would theorize. "Your mind must shine brighter than the city's light, if you wish to overcome it." Those were the last words she retained from her cousin as he too flew away into the sunset.

Farai stared at the wings of her mother and father and remembered her larvahood journeys with them through the ponds and bushes of Mutare. The memory unleashed more wise words that were buried in her mind. She remembered her father's speech: "There comes a moment in every mosquito's life when they will come face to face with the ultimate decision. If the Divine Molder intended for you to walk a narrow and straight path, you would have been molded an ant. Take a look at the challenging journey of the caterpillars. They crawl through many trials and tribulations until they reach their tree of choice. One could also argue that it is the tree that calls for the caterpillar through life's unspoken language, and propels its journey.

"Once that journey is reached, the caterpillars are rewarded the ability to fly, and no longer have to be victimized by the crawling predators they faced and avoided along their treacherous journey. But here is a secret to life; the predators only get bigger and wiser. Now as butterflies, they must be wary of larger predators with larger wings and sharper beaks. This is only one of life's many riddles and lessons to remind us that we do exist in its woven web. One hidden ripple can cause a chain reaction to affect an entire ecosystem.

"The Divine Molder has it all figured out in a strange kind of way. It's an unspoken language that speaks through our actions. If your destiny is to be smashed on the arm of a two-legger, then meet your destiny with dignity and self-worth. You wouldn't starve to death to avoid being squashed, would you? Life is filled with obstacles and challenges, so enjoy your life and all the secrets it offers to share." Those words penetrated in Farai's mind. As a larva, she didn't understand them in their full depth, but she was beginning to find meaning to them.

She zoned back to reality and began packing her belongings for the journey. Taking one last look at her birthplace, she smiled, flapped her wings continuously as to check if they were still working, and soared into the reddish sunset like so many mosquitoes before her.

*

Farai's journey to the city flowed steady, swift and undisturbed. She listened carefully to the many voices steering her from within. At the shadow hours, she rested cautiously beneath leaves and stared at the many faces of the moon. During the morning fogs, she supped carefully on the legs of zebras and wildebeests, while snacking on the necks and backs of sleeping lions and leopards for supper. She read the signs concealed in the landscape of trees, which gave warning to the path of the city. She knew that the city of Harare was drawing near. The once clean oxygen-filled countryside air became cloudy with pollution. *This must be the bad breath of the city so many have spoken about,* she thought to herself.

Farai knew that she reached the city when she landed on the roof of a car, extending her proboscis to taste the blood of what she believed was a strange looking creature. To her surprise, her proboscis was not able to penetrate through the hard shell of this uncanny moving creature. She had to learn quickly and she did. She vowed to stay away from these unnatural moving objects that carried within them the two-leggers. The moving creatures were everywhere, and this sight confirmed that she had reached the heart of the city. It was a new world to her curious imagination, and it was busy with movements and strange life forms. She saw insects of all wings, colors, and creeds. She even witnessed insects she has never encountered before. She knew that she was out of her natural element and needed to proceed with caution.

Everything around her moved at a fast pace. She found a place of comfort, stood at the edge of a bush, and stared at the moving city while readjusting her observation. She looked around for anything of familiarity to assure that she would not become a casualty to the radiant energy of confusion that stood before her. More importantly, she did not want to be lost in the wilderness of the city's den.

She retrieved Mukai's directions from her wing pocket to become more familiar with her locality. Just as she unfolded it, the heavy wind that followed a moving truck snatched the small piece of leaf from her hand and danced wildly with it in the middle of a busy street. Her natural instinct jerked her body to go after the leaf, but she immediately regained control of herself. She listened and surrendered to the voice inside of her that warned her to stay put. She stood still and watched her only map of the city sailing aimlessly in traffic like a plastic bag trapped in a heavy windstorm. Fear began to lodge itself into her mind. *Where am I to go for help?* she thought to herself. The panic alarm began to ring loudly as she trembled with fear.

She heard a soothing voice channeling from within, commanding her to breathe and stay calm. She listened and took a few deep breaths to re-welcome her peace. She then looked around to investigate her surroundings. Right above her was an old pregnant spider occupying the branch on a tree. The spider appeared to be wrapping a meal brought to her by the same wind that carried away Farai's map. Farai remembered the words of her elder Mukai, warning her of the importance of safety and the many distractions and diversions that she would encounter. She also stamped in her mind the startling statistic of the thousands of mosquitoes that lost their lives every hour of the day in the metropolis. Farai quickly came back to her senses, collected herself from the arms of fear and refocused on her mission.

She asked the spider if she could point to her the path of the great oracle.

The spider responded, "Are you referring to the wise Queen Bee of Harare."

"Yes", replied Farai.

The spider asked Farai to come closer to her web so she could show her the exact directions, using her web as the city streets.

Warning alarms rang inside, as Farai kindly rejected the offer. She informed the spider that she did not make plans to become her supper, but only sort the address.

The spider warned Farai that she had many arms, and that when she began to point her towards the direction, it would potentially confuse her.

Farai replied that she would rather chance with confusion than death. Farai maintained her distance and asked the spider to proceed with the directions.

The spider began moving her many arms in various directions, which confused Farai as she predicted. Farai thanked the spider and proceeded down the path the spider pointed with her first arm. Farai flew for a few blocks to sort an insect that was less threatening, and ask for directions. A few feet from her, two flies were holding hands and locked in the hidden language of love. She made an attempt to get their attention to ask for directions to the Queen.

"Excuse me beautiful couple," Farai yelled, and grabbed their attention. "I'm trying to find Beehive Number Seven. Can you kindly point me in that direction?"

The male fly took this moment to impress his girlfriend. He replied with hints of comical sarcasm and rudeness, "My my my, just what we need in our great city. Another bloody lost mosquito." His girlfriend snickered at this joke. "Don't you bloodsuckers know anything, or do you hatch as larvae directionally impaired?"

Trying to avoid confrontation, Farai replied, "I'm sorry for bothering you and your lovely wife; I'm just trying to get some simple directions. Are you or are you not able to help me?"

The fly replied, "The directions cannot be that simple if you're asking me." His girlfriend chuckled louder to his jokes, encouraging him on. "It is right around the corner from here, you long lipped dodo," he continued. His girlfriend laughed hysterically at the insults he was throwing at Farai.

Farai ignored the fly and continued forward to the destination he pointed her to. She could still hear him yelling insults as she flew away.

Once away from the fly, she took a few minutes to reassemble her thoughts. She tried hard not to allow the fly's ignorance to engulf her spirit. She took a few deep breaths as commanded by her inner voice. *I'm around the corner from the oracle,* she thought to herself. *I must locate a small pond to shower and gather myself.* She spotted a small pond a short distance away and stopped for a drink of water and made preparations to meet the Queen.

While rinsing her body in the small pond, ripples began to form in the water. She felt the water vibrating, and the ripples grew larger. She looked around trying to assess and understand this strange phenomenon. Fear crept back inside of her. She could see the twirls and ripples moving fast, followed by the loudest and most maddening sound she had ever heard. She covered her ears and hid for shelter beneath a small bush near the pond. To her surprise, she was met with an older grasshopper in the same position with his hands covering his ears. She asked the grasshopper in a frightening and panicky tone to explain what and where the loud sound was coming from. "Why is the water restless?" she asked. "What is happening here?"

The old grasshopper immediately recognized that Farai was new to the city, and gestured with his hand for her to stay calm. He directed his hands up and down to help her breathe and regain her peace. "Relax, young mosquito," said the grasshopper. "It's not that serious. That sound came from the airplane that just flew above us. There is an airport about a half mile away, and the plane is preparing to land."

Farai replied, "Airplane? ... Airport? What... what is that?"

The grasshopper answered, "Did you see the shadow that flew over the water? That shadow came from an airplane." After studying the confusion on Farai's face, the grasshopper gave up on trying to explain. "You must be really new to this city. Where are you from?"

Farai answered, "I'm from a small bush in Mutare."

The grasshopper stared in amazement. "Mutare," he repeated. "You're a looooong way from the bush. What are you doing out here?"

Farai explained that she arrived to city a few hours earlier to search for the oracle.

"The Queen?" the Grasshopper interrupted.

Farai replied, "Yes, the Queen, do you know of her?"

"Of course I do," spoke the grasshopper with chipper in his voice. "Every insect in this country knows the Queen. She can see the past, the future, and help to crack the hidden codes of the present." The grasshopper continued, "You must take heed to her warning. Do not take anything she says for granted. She speaks in parables, which will begin unraveling as the days carry on. She can bend worlds and speak to the other side. The things she shares may appear far-fetched, but trust me, she knows what she is talking about. Listen carefully and closely to everything she chooses to share."

Farai nodded with appreciation. She replied, "I hear that she is around the corner from this pond."

"Which pond?" the grasshopper asked.

Farai pointed to the direction of a tree as given to her by the fly.

"No, no, no," the grasshopper interrupted. "Please avoid that tree at all cost. It is a hangout for the flies. They will find ways to scam you. They take advantage of many travelers in route to the Queen. I'm glad the airplane brought you to me. There is no telling where you would have ended up playing in that flytrap." The grasshopper giggled at his joke. "You are near to the Queen," he continued, "but it is not that tree where the flies are."

The grasshopper hopped to the top of the tree above the bush and Farai followed. Once he made it to the top of the tree, he pointing to a set of trees a short distance away. "Do you see those mango trees?" he asked

Farai replied, "The one by the Litchi tree?"

"Yes," the grasshopper answered. "Queen Hive Number Seven is the seventh tree to the right of the mango tree. You'll know you are there by the growing presence of bees." He continued, "She's heavily guarded. Be respectful and everything will be ok."

Farai thanked the grasshopper, and prepared to take flight to the Queen's hive.

"Ahhh, don't worry about it," said the Grasshopper. "You know where it is at now, so try not to get lost this time. If you find yourself confused or lost again, word to the wise, never ask a fly." The grasshopper burst out with laughter at his own advice and hopped away talking to himself.

Farai flew toward the direction provided by the grasshopper. As she reached near the mango tree, she noticed the area was swarming with bees. She moved amongst the bees with caution and attempted not to interrupt or disturb their natural order.

Three bees greeted Farai. The first bee asked in a calm voice, "Is there something we can assist you with?" As Farai collected her thoughts and prepared to answer the first bee's question, the second bee interrupted her with another question. His voice was deeper than the first bee, and straight to the point. "Who sent you here?"

Farai looked back and forth between the two bees and with nervous tension in her leg. She took a few deep breaths to remain calm. The third bee interjected before she could say a word. "Who are you here to see and who are you working for?"

Farai answered calmly, "I am the daughter of Scova and Farirai. I come from the bush of Mutare to speak with the Great

Oracle. I come alone and in peace. I'm just searching for a few answers to life's many puzzles."

The bees looked at each other, then glanced back at Farai. They quickly formed a small huddle a few inches away from her to discuss their observation. "What's the assessment on this situation?" asked the first bee to the other two.

The third bee replied, "Her eyes appeared genuine, and I didn't detect any level of fabrication in her energy wave. She seems sincere in her request."

The second bee shared his assessment, "Her tiny wings, legs and arms trembled a little, but I'm sensing it was caused by her nervousness."

The first bee took another glance at Farai then gave the order to the other two bees. He commanded the second bee to take Farai with him to the Queen's entrance. He commanded the third bee to stay out of sight, but keep a keen eye on the little mosquito.

The bees broke out of the huddle and flew in different directions. The second bee signaled for Farai to follow him. Farai followed the bee while observing the unique lifestyle of the bees. The second bee signaled for Farai to pay attention and told her to stop allowing her eyes to wonder. He cautioned Farai to be respectful to the Queen. He continued, "When you meet the queen, bow your head, and wait until she asks you to come near her. Whatever you do, do not touch the Queen. If you are prepared to be stung by three hundred thousand bees, then ignore my orders. Do you understand?"

"Yes," replied Farai.

The bee continued, "If I see or even feel any signs of foul play, not only will you taste an early grave, we will send an army of killer bees to eradicate your entire village in Mutare. Do you understand?"

"Yes sir," replied Farai.

The bee led her to the front entrance of the hive and flew away. When Farai landed on the hive's main entrance, just as she was about to take her first step inside the hive, two huge bumblebees greeted her at the entrance to block her from entering.

With heavy bass in their voices, the bumblebees spoke in unison. "How may we help you? What are you doing here?"

Farai replied in a timid and nervous tone, "Um, um, I'm here to see..."

"Speak up," the bumblebee to the right of her interjected. "Does a flea have your tongue?"

Farai began to stutter as she answered, "I...I came from the bush of Mutare to see the Great Oracle Queen."

"Who led you to this hive?" asked the bumblebee to the right.

Farai continued, "I was met by three bees when I entered Bee City, and one of the three led me here."

"Did you come alone?" asked the bumblebee to the right.

Farai replied, "yes, sir."

"Put your hands up," demanded the bumblebee to the left.

Farai lifted her little arms as the bumblebees proceeded to search her pockets for their Queen's safety. After patting her down, the bumblebee to the left ordered Farai to walk straight down and stop at the front entrance of Room 7.

Farai inhaled deep, and released a big sigh as she began walking slowly towards the room. She took her time to glance at all the pictures on the hallway wall. She saw pictures of many insects, including members of her family posing with the Queen. She saw the picture of her favorite cousin Tapiwai and her uncle Tawana.

When she entered room number 7, there was a dim candle burning in the center of a table. The aroma of sweet incense filled the room. There was a soothing melody playing in the background of the hive. A soft voice traveled from behind a velvet purplish curtain.

"Sit down, Farai," the queen ordered. "I've been expecting you."

Farai was shocked to know the Queen knew her name, and immediately got down on her knees in bow as was instructed to do by the first set of bees. "You may be seated," repeated the Queen. "Please, take small sips of the warm honey water on the table."

Farai sat down on the table and began sipping the honey water. She continued to glance around at the beautiful artifacts and colors that surrounded the room. She was in awe by how warm and comfortable she felt.

Finally the Queen walked into the room. She bowed at Farai and proceeded towards the table and joined her for honey water. "I can feel all of your good energy radiating from your body," the Queen added as she sat down. "I sense you are here for clarity?"

"Yes," replied Farai. "The elder Mukai informed me that I should seek advice from you, and boasted of how insightful you were in helping her make her transition in clarity."

"Ahhh, the great Mukai," the Queen replied. "Does she still wear the gold band around her hair?" she asked.

Farai replied in a smiling tone, "Yes, she does, but it is full of grays now." They laughed together for a few seconds.

The Queen Bee continued, "Ok, Farai, now that the ice is melted and your spirit is warmer, please share that which troubles your spirit."

Farai began unveiling her story. "A few weeks ago, I had a burning desire to want more from life. This yearning caused me to question everything. Suddenly the happy world that my father once shared began to fade away. I found myself questioning my very own existence. Life from the eyes and lungs of a mosquito was no longer appealing to me."

She paused and looked at the Queen, awaiting her response.

The Queen said nothing.

She put her hands on the table and signaled for Farai's hand. Farai hesitated, recalling the warning and threat that was expressed by the other bees about touching the queen. "Don't worry about the killer bees," the Queen mentioned as if reading her thoughts. "I already sent the signal to them to stay put."

Farai sighed for relief as she lifted her hands and placed them in the palm of the Queen's hand.

The Queen asked that Farai continue with her story.

Farai did as she was ordered. She picked up the story where she left off and bombarded the Queen with lots of questions: "What was the plan of the Divine Molder when he designed my species? What purpose do I play in the blueprint of existence? Why would I be molded to bring an itchy misery upon the creatures on this planet? Why must my fate lie in the path of my feeding? Next to the roaches, fleas, and flies, my species is the most hated on the planet. This is not a proud label to carry around." She continued. "Even the insects around me look down upon me and treat me as if I'm inferior to them. I don't see a true purpose to my life or the role of my species."

Farai continued in her rant, "The elders warn the youth to stay away from the city and not become as those that flew to the light. But we yearn for adventure. We yearn for pride in a world where we do not find our purpose."

Farai paused. After observing the silence of the Queen, she continued, "I know I'm ranting and chatting away, but all I'm really saying is that I want to find my true purpose in this life."

The Queen let go of her hands and held Farai's proboscis with both of her hands. "Close your eyes and envision a light around your heart," ordered the Queen. "Focus on this light, for you will see faces of your present and past. You will hear voices of your ancient elders. Listen closely to what they have to share, and it is not for you to repeat."

Farai did as she was ordered. She closed her eyes and proceeded with the instruction given by the Queen. Darkness filled her vision, with a small light shining in the center. She focused on that light, as it grew wider.

Suddenly she felt warmth enveloping her body. Before she knew it, she was back in the bush of Mutare. She saw faces of her cousins, uncles and father. She saw her delighted mother smiling at her, and her great grandmother's old and wrinkled smile. She smiled with excitement and greeted her departed family members. She could hear their voices clearly as they laughed and rejoiced.

Next, she saw herself flying between the bushes of Mutare over her family's pond with her father, grandfather, uncle and cousin Tapiwai. She felt as if she were both an observer and a participant in the experience. The feeling of euphoria hijacked her body to replace the turmoil that once resided there.

Her father Scova greeted her with a warm hug and said, "I miss you. You are growing into a beautiful mosquito. You now carry the torch of many generations in your hand. Carry it with honor. Be proud, be loved, be yourself. While you are in Harare, please visit my friend Nam..." Farai didn't catch the full name and asked her father to repeat it. Before her father could say another word, he slowly faded away.

As her father was fading to her left, her cousin Tapiwai yelled her name to grab her attention to her right. "What's up, cousin?"

"Where did my father go?" asked Farai.

"Don't worry, Farai. He's safe and flies with you daily. Everything is going to be ok," he reiterated to help her to remain calm. "Like your eyes are round, the earth is round, everything moves in full circle." Quickly changing the subject, Tapiwai demanded that Farai visit the Chikafu Cafe to get a portrait he left for her. "Your father gave me this portrait to bring to you, but I never made it back to Mutare. The fast pace of the city lured me in, and eventually trapped me." Tapiwai continued, "I know you will love the portrait. It will give you good flashbacks of the days we swam in the family pond. It's next to the bathroom in the...." His tone became very low and slowly faded away with his body.

As Tapiwai faded into the light, her uncle Tawana caught her attention. He flew patiently to her right, waiting to share words with her. Like the philosopher he was, he spoke and went straight to the point, "Farai, don't be blinded by the lustering city lights. Don't let them intimidate you and steal your shine. Do not allow them to overpower your inner light. Like water moves in ebb and flow and eventually merges with its oneness, so does light. This is why we are so drawn to it. Those bright lights in the city can hypnotize you. The lights inside of us become attracted to the light outside of us, and they crave to meet. We are mere casualties caught in the crossfire of the higher and lower elements--love and war. Remember, there is hot and cold water, but you bathe in the warm middle. Like water flows down many streams of our bodies and the earth's body to meet, the same theory is applied to light energy. There's good light, and not so good light. Just stay in the balance of the middle."

While Farai was ingesting all that was being shared by her uncle, he changed the subject to get in the last words before he vanished. "While you are in the city, visit an elder name Nahmu at the Chamarin bar. He'll tell you more about your father." He continued, "While at the bar, please refrain from partaking the blood of any two-leggers sitting on the barstools. As tempting and easy as they may seem, do not, I repeat, *do not* consume of their blood after they drink from the bottle. If you're hungry, catch a two-legger before they drink." Her uncle Tawana waved her goodbye and began to fade away.

She was left with her grandfather, grandmother and mother. They made eye contact and stared in silence at one another. In her grandmother's eyes, she read many signs and stories. She nodded her head at mother Farirai and before she could say a word, Farai was awaked by the sudden jerk from the Queen as she released her proboscis. Farai looked around frantically and asked, "What happened? Where was I? How long was I asleep?"

The queen replied, "You were not asleep. You were away for a couple of hours."

Farai asked the Queen, "Did you see and hear all of the things that were said?"

The Queen reminded Farai that the messages shared were only for her soul. She continued, "Please ponder on the information given to you by your ancestors, while I step away for a second." The Queen removed herself from the table and headed towards the curtains from which she arrived.

Farai dwelled through her thoughts, trying to piece together all that was shared.

The Queen returned to the room with two cups of honey water. She sat them down on the table and proceeded. Her tone of voice changed as if she was being channeled by something beside herself. She proceeded, "A daunting task was ingrained on the crust of your antenna. Your destiny is marked with a mission unlike any I have witnessed."

Farai stared at her with a puzzled look. "What do you mean?" she asked.

"Shhhhhh," the Queen insisted softly. "Just listen." She continued, "You've been assigned a great mission. The future of your species and every other insect species in this country rests upon you fulfilling your mission."

Farai began to doubt what she was hearing in her thoughts.

"Remove the doubt that's swimming through your thoughts, and listen with your heart," suggested the Queen. She continued, "Fulfilling your destiny will determine the future of every living insect in this country."

Farai asked hesitantly, "What is this destiny that you speak of?"

The Queen replied, "I can not answer that, my child. Your ancestors gave you the hidden keys needed to guide you. But what I will demand of you is that you fly each day with great pride and purpose. Be proud of your molding, for the Divine Molder molds not in error. For the entire week, allow yourself to be led by the spirit of those that flew before you. Let the voices of your ancestors guide you upon your journey."

For the next hour, the Queen shared stories of a hidden ripple that binds the earthly family into one. She shared the story of a lonely leaf unaware of its purpose while approaching the gripping clutch of fall season, and how the wind rescued the leaf from its eternal demise. She told the story of a grandmother that spoke to her granddaughter through the veil of death by way of seven dresses. She explained how the seven dresses represented the seven colors of the rainbow, the seven personalities of the world, the seven days of creation, and Hive Number Seven. She told the story of a special gift that was passed through generations, and how one prodigal offspring shunned himself from the gift, and became the casualty of life's cruel hands. She followed that with a story of a vulture that refused to take heed to life's hidden codes and became a victim of its own gluttony. Finally, she shared the story of an extermination that occurred to a species of roaches that hesitated to expand beyond their comfort zone.

The queen tied all of the stories to Farai's search for her purpose and reminded her that life always leaves clues for her children to follow. When the child of life refuses to accept the path predestined, they ripple as examples from generation to generation until the path chosen is corrected.

The Queen spoke in a soft tone, "You are a leaf in the wind, Farai. Ask not of the force that guides the wind, but sail forward to your destination with pride. The answers you search for are inside of you. When you move with pride and purpose, you unleash a chemical within, that is also commanded to serve a greater cause. Find the keys within you. Listen to the voices that guide you." The Queen removed herself from the table, grabbed Farai's hand to draw her into a hug. "Fly with purpose, Farai, and your destiny will meet you."

*

Farai exited the hive with hundreds of thoughts colliding inside of her mind. She reflected on her experience to recall all that was shared by the Queen and her ancestors. Their voices resonated deep in her conscience. "Where do I begin? Where do I go?" Farai rested on the limb of a strong branch near the mango tree to collect her thoughts. She stood still in meditation to help her prioritize all that was shared throughout the meeting.

While in her meditative state, the picture of an elder mosquito and a bar appeared in her vision. She suddenly remembered the comments made by her uncle Tawana as she returned to her conscious state. "I must go to visit Nahmu at the Chamarin bar."

She spotted a work crew of ants moving a rock and asked them for directions to the bar. They all pointed her west and then proceeded back to work. Farai flew towards the bar with a new sense of purpose. She now believed in herself, and felt a sense of urgency for her mission. She realized that she had an important task to fulfill, but still was unsure of it completely. She carried no more fear.

She asked every insect in her path, but the fly for direction to the Chamarin bar. She finally arrived at the bar.

She realized that she had not eaten all day, and all the flying made her hungry. She remembered her uncle's warning about not drinking the blood from any two-legger on the barstool. She entered the bar through a crack in the main door and flew towards the ceiling to avoid being detected. She combed every inch of the bar in search of the elder Nahmu.

Suddenly, the door burst open and crashed into the wall with heavy force. The commotion commanded her attention. She looked for the signs to assure that she did not miss anything. A chubby and bald two-legger entered the bar rudely and headed toward an empty barstool. Farai quickly headed for this man and found a feasting ground behind his ears. She supped until she was full. She was sure to finish her meal before he sipped from the bottle as her uncle warned.

She made her way back to the ceiling and proceeded to scout the room for the elder Nahmu. She located an older mosquito on the third shelf behind a whiskey bottle. She flew to the direction and noticed an entire section filled with drunken mosquitoes. She greeted the elder and asked if he knew of a mosquito name Nahmu.

"You're talking to him," replied Nahmu. "How can I assist you? Are you a heavy drinker or a softy?"

"I don't drink," replied Farai. "I came here in search of another mission."

"Whatever mission you're in search of can wait," replied Nahmu. "Let me remind you that you are in a bar," he said sarcastically.

Farai interrupted, "I've been told that you are the flying map of Harare. You know every corner of the city like the back of your wings."

"Well, not every corner," Nahmu answered with a smirk on his face. "But I know enough to move around a little bit. "What are you looking for?"

Farai responded, "I'm looking for a pool in the heart of the city where the elder Scova met his destiny."

"Scova," Nahmu looked up to ponder the name. "Yes," he nodded his head slowly, "I remember the elder Scova, and he was a very wise mosquito. How did you hear of the elder Scova? You seem so young."

"He was my father," Farai replied.

"Scova was your old mosquito?" Nahmu asked as he grabbed Farai's face to get a closer look at her features. After studying her face for a few seconds, Nahmu continued. "I see you both have the same eyes. You know your old mosquito inspired many in these parts. His transition was a sad day in these valleys. He used to hold his Alcoholics Anonymous classes in a little section of the Sushuwa pool. The pool is not too far from the Benul restaurant on the eastern part of the city. If you go there tomorrow and talk to any older mosquito out there, they will tell you more about your father.

"Sushuwa pool is about two hours away. The local mosquitoes call it Blood Paradise. It's one of the only places in this city where a mosquito can sup in peace without fear of death. I see that you just ate, but by noon tomorrow, you should have your appetite back."

Farai hung with the elder Nahmu the entire night as they spoke about her father and many signs to avoid in the city. Nahmu gave her pointers on what insects to evade while in the city, and how to escape meeting an early demise. The two mosquitoes talked the night away.

When the sun shone its bright eyes upon the world, Farai began her flight to Blood Paradise. She rested along the way and utilized the keen knowledge shared by Nahmu.

Farai arrived at the destination by noon as Nahmu predicted. Her banded abdomen was empty and hunger began to call her body for blood. She surveyed the canvas that she'd been taught was a mosquito's heaven, and she became a true believer. All around her were two-leggers who appeared to be bathing in the sun near the pool. They all were almost naked with only a few articles of clothing and black glass to cover their eyesight. She took her chances and headed quickly towards her feast. Remembering the story of the vulture, she regained control of her hunger so she wouldn't be guided by her abdomen desires.

Farai cautiously explored her surroundings and swooped down onto the legs of a female two-legger. A scent poured from the woman's pores that was too strong for Farai to bear. She flew away from the two-legger to catch her breath. She returned to try again, this time holding her nose as she proceeded to sup, but she could taste the strong scent in the two-legger's blood. She flew away to focus on another victim. She landed on the hairy back of a chubby and bald two-legger. He appeared a much easier target. He didn't reek with the distasteful smell of the female two-legger.

She filled her abdomen and flew in the shadows of a litchi tree to stay beneath the radar of onlookers. She scanned the area to find an older mosquito with knowledge of her father. She spotted four middle-aged misquotes hanging out in broad daylight near a tree and flew to greet them.

Farai interrupted their conversation asking if they had heard of the name Scova. Three of the four mosquitoes shrugged their shoulders. The last of them, an outspoken mosquito, answered in a slick response, "I know of the name, but what do I get in return?"

Farai stared at him clueless and confused.

He repeated himself after noticing Farai's baffled appearance, "If I told you what I knew about Scova, what would you be willing to give me?"

Farai just stared in a bewildered manner, not understanding his lingo or frame of logic. She was unfamiliar with his demeanor and body language. She had never seen a mosquito behave and speak in this manner.

She asked in a genuine and curious tone, "What are you talking about? What do you mean?"

The mosquito replied, "We live in a capitalist jungle, sweetie. If I give you something, then I expect something in return. You can't get something for nothing out here, what kind of society do you live in?"

The other mosquitoes chuckled and appeared amused by this verbal exchange.

Farai replied with slight frustration in her tone, "What ever happened to sharing from the compassion of your heart? What about helping your fellow mosquito because they are in a state of need? Where and how did you develop such a selfish attitude?"

The mosquito replied, "I don't know what small world you flew from, but survival is the code of the city.

Farai, sensing that the conversation was pointless continued, " I don't have anything to give. "

"Then go and fly somewhere else with your big bubble eyes," the mosquito replied rudely.

The rest of mosquitoes began laughing at Farai.

Farai flew away slightly disturbed, but refused to allow anyone or anything to distract her from her mission. She remembered the Queen's warning of what happens when one becomes misaligned with his or her purpose. She recalled the story of the two-legger that chose to suppress his inherited gift to be remolded by the social norms of society.

She pitied those mosquitoes dangling like loose threads in life, unaware of their inherited potential and power.

An older mosquito named Samson observed the verbal interaction from a branch on the bush near the tree, and quickly came to Farai's aid. "Did I just hear you mention the name of the wise Scova?" he asked.

"Yes," replied Farai excitedly.

Samson continued, "Scova was my close and good friend. We flew these pools together a few seasons back. We were trying to get all these young punks off of drugs," signaling Farai's attention to the crew of middle-aged mosquitoes. "They carry with them no sense of dignity. Look at them imitating the ways of flies. They are a disgrace to our entire mosquito species."

After venting his feelings for a few minutes, Samson refocused his attention back to Farai. "How did you hear about Scova? I thought his name and memories passed with the seasons," said Samson.

Farai responded, "Scova is my father."

Samson took a double look at Farai. "Your father! Are you Farai?" he asked in a compelling tone.

"Yes," she replied.

Samson flew from the shadow of the bush to an open space and yelled from the top of his lungs to the sky, "Scova, I found her."

To the other insects who witnessed this scenario, Samson appeared to be a crazy drunken mosquito.

Farai stared at him with a sigh of relief. She knew she had found the mark to bring her one step closer to reaching her destiny.

Samson returned, "Wow, I cannot believe that I'm standing here talking to you. Your father spoke so much of you. He always said that since you were a larva, he saw and felt something special whenever he looked into your eyes. Look at you now. You look good, healthy, and definitely a chip off your old mosquito's gene pool."

Farai smiled at the complements.

Changing the subject, Samson continued, "You know he left a portrait for you with his nephew Tapiwai. Tapiwai left it at Chikafu Cafe before he was drawn to his destiny. I kept the portrait for you, hoping to one day muster enough energy and strength to carry it to you in Mutare. I'm an old mosquito now and can't fly the distance I use to."

Farai said nothing, but smiled. She shared in the excitement of Samson, and felt a bit closer to her full discovery. A sense of relief took over her body. She felt the joy of a thousand ants stumbling upon a deserted picnic. She felt like a fly caught in a bathroom stall at an all you can eat restaurant. *Finally,* she thought to herself, *finally I'm able to piece together my history and discover my true mission and life's purpose.* She hung a satisfying smile on her face while Samson reminisced and shared old stories of her father's passion and character.

Samson continued with his stories: "Your father was a visionary. He was always trying to save the world. He flew from Mutare many moons ago in hopes of rescuing all the young mosquitoes that crossed his path. It saddened him to see them constantly being swallowed by the alluring energy of the city. He started a program aimed at catching those young mosquitoes arriving to the city from bushes all over this country. Not everyone could appreciate the serenity of the countryside," he continued. "When we reach that Age of Wings, we search for our identity and it draws us to this place of spiritual mayhem. This is a cycle many insect species encounter as well. It's not only unique to mosquitoes, but to all species. Your father believed that this Age of Wings also affects the two-leggers. Look around you," he continued.

"Your father shared with me a unique theory he was developing. He believed that what is happening in our small reality is a replica of what is happening in the greater cosmos. He believed that the younger species of the giant two-leggers are also struck with the same curiosity to explore the greater world. They too share in the desire and temptation to leave their nest for the city. He believed that the young offspring of the two-leggers run to the metropolis like ours, and they too become the casualties of bars, drugs and sex. Your dad informed me that he knew this theory to be true because he rested in the backpack of a younger two-legger as he journeyed to the city.

"Rather than taking a three-day flight into the city, he preserved his energy and time by allowed the young two-legger to become his chauffeur. Your father overheard the younger two-legger conversing about heading to the city, and decided to hide in his backpack. The younger two-legger came from Nyazura, a town not far away from Mutare. Your father observed this young bright giant slowly degenerate into a drug addict and alcoholic. Your father got an opportunity to register all of the different drugs and their effects on the two-leggers' and mosquitoes' bodies with first-hand knowledge.

"As he supped on the young two-legger, the drugs and alcohol affected him. He kept a catalog of each alcohol by reading the labels on the bottles and a description of the drugs the young two-legger was taking. He kept a log on the different places the two-legger visited. He marked those places as areas of high substance risk and challenged the younger mosquitoes to avoid those places at all times.

"The young two-legger was used as his case study. He knew that the lifecycle of this young giant would unlock a solution to how we could maneuver through the metropolis. He expressed sadly how the young two-legger arrived to the city looking for work and was sidetracked by the magnetic lights and confusion like so many of our young mosquitoes. He observed the two-legger reaching out for help, but no trustful hand was there to help pull him up. All of his loved ones were back in the countryside.

"Observing this cycle of slow degeneration unlocked a key in your father's mind. This motivated him to develop a program for our young that are flying into this city in search of themselves. Your father dedicated his life trying to make it easier for the younger mosquitoes to function and be aware while living in the city. He started a substance abuse recovery program to help those mosquitoes recover from the drugs they had become addicted to while feeding off of the two-leggers roaming through streets and bars.

"Your father was the first to develop a program that helped the mosquitoes identify patterns and behaviors of the two-leggers."

Farai soaked in all the knowledge and information she was hearing for the first time about her dad. It made her proud to be her father's larva. Her smile was plastered on her face as she followed the elder Samson to the Benul restaurant to pick up the portrait left by her father. Samson shared many more stories. Like a three thousand page book, he went on and on. Some stories were sad and generated tears in Farai's eyes, while others were funny and filled her with laughter. She finally had the opportunity to learn who her father really was. This helped her to understand the many different layers hidden within herself.

The many questions that once swam through her childhood thoughts were being answered. As he spoke of her father, he was unknowingly unveiling the hidden layers of her purpose. The more the elder Samson spoke, the better the understanding she gained of the world and herself.

When they arrived at the restaurant, the elder Samson led her to a table occupied by a strange looking couple. The female species of the giant two-legger wore a bright red hat filled with feathers plucked from different species of birds in the area. The male species appeared shorter and plump in stature compared to the woman. His features seemed very familiar.

The elder Samson called for Farai's attention and she followed him to a safe pathway beneath the table of the strange couple. While the elder surveyed the four corners beneath the table for the hidden portrait, Farai took the opportunity to sup on the ankles of the male and followed with the woman. The elder Samson signaled her to come to the left corner beneath the table where there was a small space that led to a room. It sat behind a piece of gum stuck under the table.

The midsize room could house four mosquitoes comfortably, and was filled with what appeared to be old junk. Samson looked at Farai and stated, "This is your father's storage. This is where he kept all of his poetry, writings, photos and unique items he had collected along his long journey. It brings tears to my eyes to see you standing in this place. Your father wished for this day," added Samson. "He knew the day would draw near, when you would make your way to the city in search of yourself. He was afraid that the city would swallow you whole, and you would fall prey to the confusion and lose your identity."

Samson pulled out a portrait from beneath a pile of old leaf. "This is the portrait your father wanted you to have. He wanted Tapiwai to bring it to you. He believed that if you could get this portrait before you entered the city, it would better prepare you on how to navigate. He was adamant about getting it to you."

On the portrait were photos of a younger Scova and her mother Farirai. Farai sat down to observe and study every inch of the portrait. It was filled with pictures, poetry and various writing on every part of it. Farai informed Samson that she would need more days to look through everything and explore all of the portraits and writings in the room. "Days," Samson replied, "this area belongs to you now. On that portrait are hidden codes that you have to decipher. This portrait is a map that was to lead here. You got here without the portrait. He decoded it in case Tapiwai got sick along the way, but if this portrait ever made it to the hands of another insect or mosquito, they would not know how to get here. He wanted to keep this place hidden for you. Take your time; for you have your entire life ahead of you. You can read all the things he studied about our species and many others. This place belongs to you," Samson repeated.

Samson left an address for Farai to visit if she ever wished to find him again. "I live in the third Litchi tree over in Blood Paradise by the pool. I must go now." He waved her goodbye as he made his way from beneath the table and flew away.

Farai stood still and explored the room for what appeared to be an eternity. She began by looking at the many pictures of her father and mother. Next, she examined the many strange items collected by her father. She then started reading through leaves of her father's poetry and writing. She gained a better understanding of her father's perspectives on life, his hidden passions and his unique sense of humor. The more Farai read, the more she learned about herself and developed clarity about her calling. The many questions that once burned inside of her unraveled with every poem she read by her father:

Purpose
Fly forward with purpose,
Above the green pasture and sleeping wildebeest.
Fly forward with purpose,
Beneath the cold moon resting in summer's east.
As the ants march to purpose,
The Bees pollinate with spring's grace.

Hidden Ripples: Purpose

As the mosquitos fly to purpose,
We teach all to respect nature with our itchy trace.

-Scova

She read poem after poem, and drew more strength from each passage. She lost and found herself between paragraphs and volumes of her father's work. It became a ritual for her. She slept, woke up, supped on a few ankles throughout the day and continued reading. She finally reached the point where she found her inner peace. Her father's work helped to inspire a new pathway within her. The veil of confusion no longer covered her eyes, and the clouds that once hid her inner sun began to dissipate. She now knew her purpose. She now knew her mission. It was as if an invisible hand drew her destiny before her eyes. She pledged to continue and fulfill the much-needed work. She knew that she was to first honor her oath by returning to Mutare and share her experience with other pupas that were destined to follow her wing pattern.

She left her father's dwelling with a new set of eyes. Her spirit now soared, and she felt apart from her flesh. She had completely lost track of time. She was not aware of how long she has been in the sanctuary. She was now ready to move on and make her mark on the world. She was prepared for the obstacles and roads that lay before her. She felt like a new butterfly whose wings had just sprouted for the new spring season. She was charged and ready for the task ahead.

She headed to Bloody Paradise to thank and state her farewell to the elder Samson. When she arrived to the Litchi tree where Samson resided, there appeared to be a lot of commotion at Bloody Paradise. There were bright lights everywhere and two-leggers were running around with all kinds of devices in their hands. She greeted Samson with curiosity in her eyes and asked about the commotion.

Samson informed her that death appeared to carry away another spirit to its wholeness. With wise words, Samson philosophized on how the state of death was the one language that all living things on the planet knew too well. He added how it was intriguing to watch the way the two-leggers dealt with death. He explained how it became some kind of weird ritual of lights that occurred when the two-leggers were carried away to journey to the other side.

As he explained his theory, he pointed to the objects before him. Pointing to an ambulance, he explained how the big glowing vehicle was a moving coffin that howled and carried the bodies away. Samson reminded Farai that even the cruel two-leggers had to answer when the grim reaper knocked.

Farai watched as an ambulance hauled away the body of a short stubby bald man. Farai's mind danced with life and death, and temptation became a luring song drawing her attention to the flashing lights. Unlike her cousin Tapiwai, she immediately regained control of herself. Driven with purpose, she vowed to never be distracted and misguided by the lights of confusion. As the sun descended to wave farewell to another day; as the ambulance howled away the corpse of a being who tasted his last day; as the city night lights came alive to draw in the souls of mosquitoes, moths and lost children, Farai decided that it was time to go back home and fulfill her purpose. Farai took one last look at the city of Harare and recited a poem for every lost mosquito...

"From ponds we fly to taste the bitter fruit,
Offering our spirits to lights without names.
Guidance lost in the wind of confusion,
Which chants falling faces around the burning flames.
For what is the path of the ant lost at desert,
Or the dragonfly lost at pond?
Still they gaze forward with pride
Ingrained with purpose from beyond."

...and flew into the sunset back to the bush of Mutare.

*

A secret delegation sat around a table to discuss the latest news. The table was filled with frowning faces as they wrestled to understand what they had just received. Their wicked plan was met with an extreme setback. This group met in the shadow of life, and believed themselves to be the caretakers of planet earth. They believed that they were ordained to help maintain balance and order on the planet.

The news of the tragedy left the table in complete silence. No one could find the words to carry on the conversation. An old cracked voice asked softly, "Who else knew the code?"

"No one," replied a man holding a newspaper with the highlighted story on the front page. "When he left, the code left with him", continued the man. "Forty years of research down the drain. We operate in secrecy and must continue to do so. Sharing the code with anyone meant that there was room for failure, and the mission would be jeopardized."

"Has he talked to anyone while there?" asked the old voice.

"We tracked his entire movement while in Zimbabwe through his passport and telephone device. We found nothing. We sent an investigation team to the region to collect the video footage to retrace his steps. According to our tracking, he landed in Harare at 23:32 and checked into the Sunbowl Hotel, the one that is surrounded by Litchi trees. Camera shows that he took a cab at 00:50 and arrived at Charmarin bar at 00:57.

"While at the bar, he purchased three Long Islands, and a few shots of tequila. He arrived back at the hotel at 02:24. We have him on camera sunbathing by the pool the next day, and later that night, he checked into the Benul restaurant. He ate a chicken and rice dish and later checked back into his room. That was the last time anybody saw him.

"The hotel clerk reported that the telephone was down that entire day, and the housekeeper found him in his bed a few days later. She reports that she avoided cleaning his room because he made a point that no one was to enter his room until he checked out. They discovered him after four days when it was time to check out. His family asked that his body be flown back home for a full investigation.

"During the autopsy, the doctor found mosquito bites behind his ears, beneath his elbows and around his left ankle. The doctors concluded that his cause of death was from Malaria. His body was unable to fight off the symptoms. As stated earlier, when he departed this planet, the code left with him. We are not sure where he left the suitcase because the heavy tree line in Zimbabwe affected the satellite service. And even if we found the suitcase, we do not know the code for getting into it, nor the code for releasing the chemical."

"So, what you are really saying is that Project: Spring Cleaning is terminated?" asked the old voice.

"Yes," replied the man, "Project: Spring Cleaning is terminated."

The chemical will not be released into the water supply. The citizens of Zimbabwe will not be affected. They can thank their local mosquito population for that.

*

The Queen Bee pulled out her little crystal and smiled, watching Farai flying freely into the sunset. "Humans, when will they learn," she muttered to herself.

Hidden Ripples: Purpose

Acknowledgements

I would like to thank my family for their unconditional love and support. Thank you all for being honest with me and keeping me grounded. A special thanks to my Aunt Lois for helping to revive my spirit while at a low point. I am forever grateful for you.

I would also like to thank my wonderful wife for standing in my corner through many obstacles and challenges. Thank you for staying close on the windy path. I'm blessed to have such a special person by my side.

Thanks to Matt, Michelle, and Grady for your support and believing in my vision. Alone, I may be able to lift a stone, but collectively, we have and will continue to move mountains.

The story *Purpose* could not have been written without the magnificent people I met in Zimbabwe and South Africa. My visit to the Southern region of Africa provided me with a deep sense of clarity. From the moment I landed in Zimbabwe, I fell in love with the spirit that occupied the land. The people I've met captured my heart and helped to draw me closer to my purpose. I am forever indebted to all of the kind, humble and warm spirits I've met along my journey. A special thanks to Nhamu, Farai, Tapiwai, Dr. Gwenzi, Ramzu and all the people I didn't mention. Thank you for the laughter, the tears, and for opening your homes and hearts to me and my brothers. Thank you all for contributing to my growth.

Lastly, I want to thank Palesa, Ande and gang, Rob (Chi), Connie, Bahle, Papi and all the wonderful people I met in South Africa. You all have helped to inspire these words and the peace I feel within.

Thank You!

About the Author

Lemuel LaRoche's work inspires, empowers and educates audiences of all ages. His mentorship and counseling helps to cultivate and enrich the opportunity for positive change in lifestyle, personal growth and communication. LaRoche earned a Master's degree in Social Work from the University of Georgia. He currently works with youth, families and communities across Northeast Georgia.

Made in the USA
Charleston, SC
23 November 2013